MY OWN LITTLE THEOSIS

(An Autobiography of Redemption)

By

Robert G. Patrick McLawhorn

1

CONTENTS   PAGE

DEDICATION

To:

God the Father, my Creator, from Whom all good things come,

God the Son, my Redeemer and Savior of my soul,

God the Holy Spirit Who sanctified me, is in all places and fillest all things, and

The Theotokos for Her constant intercessions for us sinners.

Not many people will volunteer to read a manuscript such as this one with no promise of it ever being published. Only out of great friendship and compassion did John Asturias agree to do so. Without his patient understanding with my myriad of different mood swings and encouragement, I doubt this opus would have ever been completed. This work is dedicated also to you with a most heartfelt appreciation, John.

God grant you many years.

Barkeep Gus, your kindness to me shall never be forgotten. Before your terrible accident resulting in your falling asleep in the Lord, you constantly encouraged me to keep writing and treated me with great respect despite my emotional problems. You ask me to dedicate any writing to you, with these words, "To my barkeep friend Gus." So, here is my promise kept.

Rest eternal grant unto him most compassionate Lord.

Robert Paul of Minneapolis, MN, thank you for the enormous task of reading and suggestions for revising the original book. You are greatly appreciated.

Last, but by no means least, endless thanks to Fr. Anthony Coniaris, of Life & Life Publishing, by whom had not I been <u>IN</u>spired, this book would have <u>EX</u>pired. God grant you many years.

Appreciation

Many people have patiently heard this story, some over and over again. All have encouraged me to write of my experiences, especially the stories. To all of you I extend great appreciation.

God grant you many years.

Declaration

Have mercy on me, O God, according to Thy great mercy; and according to the multitude of thy tender mercies blot out my transgressions...For I know my iniquity, and my sin is ever before me. Against Thee only have I sinned and done this evil in thy sight....

Psalm 51

Come unto me, all you who labor and are heavy laden, and I will give you rest. Take my yoke upon you, and learn from me; for I am gentle and lowly in heart, and you will find rest for your souls. For my yoke is easy, and my burden is light.

Matthew 11:28-30:

Truer words were never spoken. I personally will vouch for, and testify to, the truth and reality of Christ's tender, yet most powerful, call to us sinners. This beautiful Protestant hymn, by Will Thompson, expresses it perfectly:

> Softly and tenderly Jesus is calling,
> calling for you and for me;
> see, on the portals he's waiting and
> watching,
> watching for you and for me.
> Refrain: Come home, come home; ye
> who are weary come home;
> earnestly, tenderly, Jesus is calling,
> calling, O sinner, come home!

PREFACE

Theosis, deification, transfiguration, revelation, born again, slain by the Holy Spirit, being saved, being sanctified, converted, got religion, enlightened are many ways of expressing, by one denomination or another, the same idea: a person is filled with, or touched by, the Holy Spirit and feels great relief and pardon from sins of the past. The proof of the pudding, so to speak, is the change in behavior after the experience. A person may have great emotional experiences during a religious ceremony, or from some other cause, which is not necessarily a theosis. If it is a true theosis, then the person will have a life style change. The good person will become better and the abject sinner will have a life style change to goodness. That change is one of the most difficult accomplishments a person can do. But, with the grace of God, it can be done.

It is doubted by some theologians whether a person not of great holiness could really experience a theosis, deification, transfiguration. Without getting into extremely deep theology, there are many statements confirming the fact that we mere mortals, through the grace of God, can have such extraordinary experiences. I, for one, and St. Paul of Tarsus for another, can, and do, attest to the experience. Another well-known conversion was that of John Newton, writer of the hymn Amazing Grace. He had read the Imitation of Christ by Thomas a' Kempis so he knew intellectually what it was to be a Christian, but not in his heart. He was captain of a slave trading ship in the mid 1700s when his ship nearly founded in a storm. At that time he gave his life to Christ and eventually gave up slave trading. The hymn is the result of his theosis, and he wrote many other hymns as well. He became an Anglican priest and at 84 years old he said, "...I remember two things, that I am a great sinner and that Christ is a great Savior." John Newton and I have six things in common: 1. not of the Orthodox faith, 2. great sinners, 3. redeemed by Christ, 4. changed our lives to live for Christ, 5. Anglicans, but not regular devotees, and 6. not had all the requirements of Church association and Eucharist, in the traditional sense, supposedly required to receive this great blessing. Nevertheless, who could deny that John Newton experienced a Revelation, theosis, if a positive lifestyle change is a criterion?

That is what this book is about. Not only my experience, but changing my life style through my own little theosis showing that the God of Abraham, Isaac, Jacob, and our Redeemer Jesus is truly the God of forgiveness, mercy, and compassion.

Why take such effort to define and discuss theosis? To demonstrate that not only the great saints of the past, i.e. Moses and St. Paul, may experience it, but to show the purist, monastics, and theologians that we simple believers, and sinners, also may be filled with the Holy Spirit and experience the joys of the uncreated light of Mt. Tabor, if only a little bit. For is it not for the sick, not the healthy or the saint, but the sinner, for whom Jesus was crucified and resurrected? "...They that be whole need not a physician, but they that are sick. I am not come to call the righteous, but the sinners to repentance." St. Matthew, 9:12-13.

I will not bore the reader with 70 some years of minute details of my life. I will tell of the most dramatic high points and give indications and allusions of other events of my life. I will, however, describe the very moment of my little theosis-deification-revelation that changed my life, what some of the resultant changes were, and devoted relationships.

INTRODUCTION

Probably a more plain and direct statement could not be found concerning God's effect on a person's life than the Battle Hymn of the Republic by Julia Ward Howe in the fifth stanza. It states:

> In the beauty of the lilies
> Christ was born across the sea,
> With a glory in His bosom
> That transfigures you and me;
> As He died to make men holy,
> Let us die to make men free;
> While God is marching on.

By transfigures could she possibly have meant that the military personnel, and the civilian population, had an en mass spiritual experience that gave them a dedication to duty that they would not other wise have had. Is it not a kind of martyrdom that military personnel suffer, in the cause of freedom, when going into battle, facing the enemy face to face, to capture or be captured, to wound or be wounded, to mutilate or be mutilated, to kill or be killed at the command of higher authority? Albeit that the higher command is not always the most intelligent leaders. As she says, 'let us die to make men free.' Metaphorically speaking, could she have meant that they died in the Lord, offering their all as a sacrifice for others? Julia Ward Howe could well have meant that. She was no sniveling, dainty, airhead as usually thought of women being in the 1800s. She was highly educated, an active and strong advocate of women's rights, a Transcendentalist and highly respected by the intelligencia of her time.

Most of the major world religions affirm revelation in some sense as a basis for their doctrines and practices. Special revelation refers to the knowledge of God that comes through specific experiences, such as visions, dreams, or events [(Microsoft) (Encarta (R) 98 Encyclopedia]. The most authoritative and relevant of the many statements by Bishop Timothy Ware concerning theosis or deification in The Orthodox Church for my hypothesis is, "...deification presupposes life in the Church, life in the sacraments. Theosis according to the likeness of the Trinity involves a common life, and it is only within the fellowship of the Church that this common life coinherence can be properly realized. Church sacraments are the means appointed by God whereby we may acquire the sanctifying Spirit and be transformed into the divine likeness". (pp. 237-238) It would be difficult to justify that profound statement by Bishop Ware with John Newton, as mentioned above, and with my experience.

Further, it would be difficult to justify, by using Bishop Ware's statement, a possible theosis of some sacrificial military personnel, including firefighters and police. However, it is God's compassionate decision, not our decision, to say what is the Church and Sacraments in such times of stress when fighting for the common good. In the heat of battle, the soldiers' sense of camaraderie could be their Church, the willingness of them to give their all could be the Sacrament, i.e., the sacrificial offering. Not to be forgotten are the unsung heroes: the spouses, children, and families of those on the firing line. They, too, are passion suffers of loss. Over the years, the military has given medals, e.g., Medal of Honor, Distinguished Service Cross, and Distinguished Service Medal for gallantry, heroism, and meritorious service. (Those who have not fought in battle will not fully understand, those of us who have, will understand).

All Hands:
This is a reminder from Col Allen
Bacon. Lest we forget!
Thanks and Semper Fi, Colonel,
Seamus

This photo appeared in several places last
Friday with the caption, "U.S. Marines AND

SAILORS pray over a fallen comrade at a
first aid point after he died from wounds
suffered in fighting in Fallujah, Iraq,
Thursday, April 8, 2004." While it tells of a
poignant moment experienced by our
Marines, it does not tell the whole.story.
Notice that the individual standing second
from right has a pair of bandage scissors
and a rubber Penrose drain (used as a
tourniquet to draw blood and start IVs) in
his left breast pocket. Also, note that the
individual kneeling at right and the one
kneeling third from right are wearing rubber
surgical gloves. These personnel are
Sailors hospital corpsmen. As they have

for nearly 106 years, Navy hospital corpsmen have served alongside their Marines, sharing the risks of battle and the pain of loss.

During recent combat action in the Al Anbar Province of Iraq, HM3 Fernando Mendez died as a result of a gun shot wound while assigned to Echo Company, 2d Battalion, 4th Marines, 1st Marine Division. HM3 Mendez was assigned to 1st Marine Division as an augmentee from Naval Medical Center San Diego.

As we go about our daily business at the Navy Memorial, honoring men and women of the sea services, let us not forget that the service and sacrifice of our Marines and Sailors is not confined to the conflicts of distant history. It is lived out each day around the world.

No one veteran won the war alone. All of them fighting together, and together with those supporting the fighters, won it. To all of those who honorably served and died, from the first shot for freedom from tyranny until the last shot of the last war, we give our undying thanks for our American way of life which we enjoy.

The saying that: 'a picture is worth a thousand words' is very true, but so is 'the pen is mightier than the sword'. Sometimes words can express feelings that a picture cannot. The following words had to be written. I am not sure their sentiments could have been expressed as well in pictures.

Ben Stein

For many years Ben Stein has written a biweekly column for the online Website called "Monday Night At Morton's", from that famous restaurant which was often frequented by Hollywood Stars. Now Ben is terminating the column to move on to other things in his life. Reading his final column to our military is worth a few minutes of your time because it praises the most unselfish among us; our military personnel, others who protect us daily and portrays a valuable lesson learned in his life. (Author unknown)

...

Ben Stein's Last Column

How Can Someone Who Lives in Insane Luxury Be a Star in Today's World?

As I begin to write this, I "slug" it, as we writers say, which means I put a heading on top of the document to identify it. This heading is "e online" FINAL," and it gives me a shiver to write it. I have been doing this column for so long that I cannot even recall when I started. I loved writing this column so much for so long I came to believe it would never end. It worked well for a long time, but gradually, my changing as a person and the world's change have over taken it.

On a small scale, Morton's, while better than ever, no longer attracts as many stars as it used to. It still brings in the rich people in droves and definitely some stars. I saw Samuel L. Jackson there a few days ago, and we had a nice visit, and right before that, I saw and had a splendid talk with Warren Beatty in an elevator, in which we agreed that Splendor in the Grass was a super movie. But Morton's is not the star galaxy it was, though it probably will be again.

Beyond that, a bigger change has happened. I no longer think of Hollywood stars are terribly important. They are uniformly pleasant, friendly people, and they treat me better than I deserve to be treated. But a manor woman who makes a huge wage for memorizing lines and reciting them in front of a camera is no longer my idea of a shining star we should all look up to. How can a man or woman who makes an eight –figure wage and lives in insane luxury be a star in today's world, if by "star" we mean someone bright and powerful and attractive as a role model? Real stars are not riding around in the back of limousines or in Porsches or getting trained in yoga or Pilates and eating raw fruit while they have Vietnamese girls do their nails. They can be interesting, nice people, but they are not heroes to me any longer.

A real star is the soldier of the 4th Infantry Division who poked his head into a hole on a farm near Tikrit, Iraq. He could have been met by a bomb or a hail of AK-47 bullets. Instead, he faced an abject Saddam Hussein and the gratitude of all decent people of the world. A real star is the U.S. soldier who was sent to disarm a bomb next to a road north of Baghdad. He approached it, and the bomb went off and killed him. A real star, the kind who haunts my memory night and day, is the U.S, soldier in Baghdad who saw a little girl playing with a piece of unexploded ordnance on a street near where he was guarding a station. He pushed her aside and threw himself on it just as it exploded. He left a family desolate in California and a little girl alive in Baghdad.

The stars who deserve media attention are not the ones who have lavish weddings on TV but the ones who patrol the street of Mosul even after two of their buddies were murdered and their bodies battered and stripped of the sin of trying to protect Iraqis from terrorists. We put couples with incomes of $100 million a year on the covers of our magazines. The noncoms and officers who barely scrape by on military pay but stand on guard in Afghanistan and Iraq and on ships and in submarines and near the Arctic Circle are anonymous as they live and die.

I am no longer comfortable being a part of the system that has such poor values, and do not want to perpetuate those values by pretending that who is eating at Morton's is a big subject. There are plenty of other stars in the American firmament....the policemen and women who go off on patrol in South Central and have no idea if they will return alive. The orderlies and paramedics who bring in people who have been in terrible accidents and prepare them for surgery, the teachers and nurses who throw their whole spirits into caring for autistic children, the kind men and women who work in hospices and in cancer wards. Think each and every fireman who was running up the stairs at the World Trade Center as the towers began to collapse.

Now you have my idea of a real hero. We are not responsible for the operation of the universe, and what happens to us is not terribly important. God is real, not a fiction, and when we turn our lives to Him, he takes far better care of us than we could ever do for ourselves. In a word, we make ourselves sane when we fire ourselves as the directors of the movie of our lives and turn the power over to Him. I came to realize that life lived to help others is the only one that matters. This is my highest and best use as a human.

I can put it another way. Years ago, I realized I could never be as great an actor as Olivier or as good a comic as Steve Martin--or Martin Mull or Fred Willard—or as good an economist as Samuelson or Friedman or as good a writer as Fitzgerald. Or even remotely close to any of them. But I could be a devoted father to my son, husband to my wife and, above all, a good son to the parents who had done so much for me. This came to be my main task in life. I did it moderately well with my son, pretty well with my wife and well indeed with my parents (with my sister's help). I cared for and paid attention to them in their declining years. I stayed with my father as he got sick, went into extremis and then into a coma and then entered immortality with my sister and me reading the Psalms.

This was the only point at which my life touched the lives of the soldiers in Iraq or the firefighters in New York. I came to realized that life lived to help others is the only one that matters and that is my duty in return for the lavish life God has devolved upon me to help others He has placed in my path. This is my highest and best use as a human.

Faith is not believing that God can. It is knowing that God will.
By Ben Stein

In THE ORTHODOX CHURCH, Bishop Ware further states, "...said one of the Desert Fathers 'If it were possible for me to find a leper and give to him my body and to take his, I would gladly do it. For this is perfect love'. Such is the true nature of theosis." (pp.237). If wanting to help others to the point of sacrifice is theosis, then again I say what about military personnel giving the ultimate sacrifice to save our American heritage and comrades-in-arms, is that acceptable as theosis?. After all, since those heroic military troops could have disserted, but did not, are they then passion bearers? Are those who were injured and suffered but survived any less heroic? In the field of safety, it is taught that the severity of the accident is a matter of chance. The accident itself is a matter of relationships, or rather malfunction of relationships, between man, machine and environment. Therefore, whether a soldier is killed or injured, the bravery of being there is the same. It is not important what their moral lives might have been or not have been before or after the moment of truth. At the moment of truth, their moral courage to sacrifice their lives for their country and comrades-in-arms was their call to duty (theosis?), and they persevered. Thus, the result of suffering or dying for others can be transfiguration-deification-theosis-revelation.

Our Lord, being wholly man as well as wholly God, set the precedence of human transfiguration on Mt. Tabor, and showed that man, even mortal men, such as Peter, James, and John, could witness it, experience it, and survive it.

CHAPTER ONE

The Early, Early, Early Years

L ate spring and early summer, just before the oppressive humidity sets in, is a magnificent time of the year in eastern North Carolina.

THE FIELD OF MEMORIES

Small fields, between the sparse houses where I lived, are full of flowers, tall grass, and abundant diverse spider webs, which tempt this five-year-old child to touch them. Some strange feeling of caution keeps me from harm as I back away. Some of the webs are large and ziggazedly white. The spiders are large and black, as I recall. All sorts of insects are buzzing around. Ladybugs of bright orange with black spots, gorgeous multi colored Ruby Throated Hummingbirds humming around my head making ethereal music. Mysterious praying mantis poised to grab me filling me with gleeful fear. To a five-year-old, a praying mantis is a large and menacing creature from hell. It could grab you and bite your head off in one bite. All such things are enormous to a five year old boy, and as such I have an imagination unfathomable to adults, even that of the modern film makers, because in the Field of Memories everything is real. Oh, yes, and there are bees with fearful stingers, and long tongue like mouths, gathering nectar from the young flowers. They are quite colorful, beautiful, buzzing around, and mesmerizing, but all very scary. Other bees of a quite larger and different variety are buzzing around in the tall grass and flowers. They offer nectar to a youthful flowering five-year-old, not take it. Such is a large part of my youth, with one bee or another. And yet, mother reads Bible stories to me.

There were happy memories. We had a cow in the yard, in the early 1930s. My brother, just a little older than I, would squirt milk directly from the cow into my face. I had a whole neighborhood of friends with which to play hide and seek, hopscotch, and tag. Clinging to a screen door in our house was a terrifying bat. My father quickly dispatched it with an ice pick. A few years later my parents divorced. But, not after the physical fights and threats of killing us all by my father, who by then had become an alcoholic. The alcohol was, supposedly, a painkiller for the injury from WW I. Many of my grade school friends, of the affluent set, were no longer my friends because of the divorce. So were the life and times of this poor five-year-old in the early 1930s. All these incidents affected me all my life, or I should say, until later years, they controlled my life. Yes, they do still influence my decisions, but the decisions are mine and I must hold myself accountable for the behaviors resulting from those decisions. I have learned to control those behaviors by the teachings of the Church and the grace of God. 'For every success', my Mother taught me when I was a child, 'you must thank a hundred people, but for every mistake you have only yourself to blame'. A little time after the spiders and bees, perhaps two or three years, I had what might be called my first religious stirrings. I would go and sit quietly in the church (back then the Churches were always open). During one of these visits, the pastor, who later baptized me, comes sits beside me. He asks if anything is wrong and if I need help of any kind. I told him no. I am sitting here talking to God (I was not hallucinating, I meant spiritually talking to God), and because it is so peaceful and some day I hope to be a preacher like you. He gives me a blessing and walks away.

Chapter Two

The Early, Early Years

Having survived grade schools, in which I failed a couple of times and was held back (this happened to students quite frequently back then). I say grade schools, because there were two in my hometown. I started in one, I moved to the other side of town, so attended the other one. The latter one burned down, so I had to walk across town, back to the first one.

Eventually I moved on to junior high, which was in the same building as the senior high school.

Junior high school was roughly about halfway between the two grade schools. So I didn't have to walk quite as far. The school that burned down was not rebuilt before I started junior high school. I had heard a concert played by the high school band while still in grade school. No, I did not hear an out of tune, riddled with wrong notes, anticipating the beat, behind the beat, and perhaps playing a different piece of music, band. What I heard was music from heaven played by a heavenly host of God's musicians performed with perfection. I was hooked. It stirred feelings of inexpressible joy in my young heart. So the first thing I did upon arriving at junior high school was to sign up for the band. O, what joy! My mother, however, was quite pleased when I switched from taking the tuba home to practice, for the baritone horn. Enough was enough of oompa, oompa, oompa, from the tuba for that saintly woman (it is a pity indeed that Protestants don't canonize saintly people, because my mother was indeed saintly; she had to be a saint: she raised my two brothers and me).

Chapter Three

The Early Years

What stirred my young heart also, and other parts of my anatomy, was puberty. There is no need for me to state, nor do I imagine the reader needs to hear of what happened then. Suffice it to say that I had two great teachers with endless compassion to lead me on through one tempest after another. The band director and chorus teacher discerned my inner feelings and saw that music was the vehicle for which I was to find my path. I thoroughly enjoyed the football games, parades, concerts, and state competitions with the band. The chorus had concerts, state competitions, and an annual play. What a wonderful world of fantasy I lived in during those times. I learned to take barbs and darts thrown at me by other students by retreating into my world of music. The only athletic achievement at that time was to earn an American Red Cross Lifesaver Certificate. I failed a grade or two then also. The darts and barbs did their job on me. I survived, barely. I had a few close friends, neighbors mostly, with whom I played. The Boy Scouts, and the Scout Master, George Haskett (with his thrilling, chilling, scaring stories; my favorite was, as he put his fore finger on the side of his nose and make a hideous nasal sound would say, "Many come to the house of Yellow Dragon, but feeewww returned...he, he, he!—oh, how unfortunate children are today with Scifi which leaves no room for imagination within oneself; it all comes from outside of them), just like my teachers, were great experiences. All of those years are now somewhat jumbled together. It is all one mass of happinesses and sadnesses. Mental and emotional ups and downs that would exasperate and challenge even modern school counselors were my hourly companions. In other words, I was a mess! Through it all however, my mother gave me boundless love and affection. It was the summer of 1948, I was 18 years old, and still in the ninth grade. A Summer School teacher helped me pass algebra so that I could go on to the 10th grade. Still, I did not want to continue school. I auditioned for the Navy School of Music in Washington, DC, was accepted and joined the Navy. This is the end of the early years.

Chapter Four

In the Navy, in the Navy

It was August 1948. The first step to
growing up: although people like me never
actually grow up. We might slightly mature
over the years, gaining a little wisdom by
surviving one mistake after another; sometimes
making the same mistake more than once, or
even more than twice (so goes the theory of
20/20 hindsight).

Navy boot camp was the perfect place
for me, in some regards. It taught me
discipline, responsibility, and that I was not 'a
slow learner' as I was considered being in
school. I could do anything I wanted to do. I
just had to try harder and overcome my poor
self-image. There was no violence, physical or
emotional, or at least not for me there wasn't,

except what emotional burden I saddled upon myself. There was one time when I received a fairly good swift kick in the seat of my navy uniform pants. I complained about a piece of twine in my breakfast food. I never complained again. I later learned that the twine was used to hang the pork on the hook, and by some strange accident the twine got into the food. The physical exercise, drilling, marching, classes on knot tying, Navy history and Navyisms were all good for me. Some of that got me through some most difficult times in later life. Most of all, I knew that when boot camp was over I was to go to the Navy Music School in Washington, DC, which I did.

BAR-B-QUE SAUCE IN A BOTTLE

After so many weeks in boot camp training, we were allowed to go on liberty, that is, a day out off the base. Several of us went to Chicago together. Other groups of young men went to various parts of town to find that which was most pressing for their physical needs. Some of them made it quite clear what those needs were and what they were going to do

37

about it. Among the groups some were native to Chicago, or at least knowledgeable about where to find what they were looking for. My group was looking for other physical pleasures: food. We stumbled onto a restaurant advertising southern style bar-b-cue with real southern style sauce. We all being from south of the Mason Dixon Line, had to have that. While waiting for the food to come, we thought of pork roasted over an open pit, chopped into small pieces with vinegar on it. What came was a slice of pork with some kind of sauce in a bottle with a variety of spices. I asked about the authentic southern style. The answer I received was most jolting to my limited experienced mind: not everywhere in the south has the same thing. This is from the part of the south you have never been. In any case, it tasted good and I learned about bar-b-que sauce in a bottle. The first of many startling earthly revelations to come.

My first day at the music school reminded me of the first time I heard the high school band. I could hardy wait to start with a private teacher, theory classes, etc. However, the school had certain plans of which I didn't know. While waiting for enough new students to arrive to start a new class, I found myself doing the work of a janitor for about two months. But I was thrilled at hearing the others practice their instruments, and the large teachers/students band play once a week. Finally I did start my studies and graduated.

My first duty station was in Jacksonville, Florida. It was like a country club with swimming pools, palm trees, beautiful weather, and our own rehearsal hall to practice for concerts. It was only a small band, 21 of us. But we had great times. The times became too great, as this was my first time out away from home. For the first time, I drank alcohol in excess. I started smoking a year earlier in boot camp at 18 years old, and finally quit in 1988 when I was 58 years old. The beer and what ever I was drinking became my major focus in life. Fortunately, the Navy saw to it that I did have responsibilities and was forced to carry them out. Here was the place I left all my Protestantism and became a Roman Catholic. At least in the confessional and praying the Rosary I had some help with my problems, but nothing really changed, except I was given hope. Hope being birthed by desperation is a kind of salvation from hopelessness. It stays debilitating depression.

This is where I unfortunately learned to suffer what is now called codependency. What stress, agony, mental torture, identity destroying, gut wrenching, and anxiety this condition can cause; with one person or another over the next 51 years I suffered this torment. Yes, even during my marriages, but not quite as intense. After all, I did love my wives and had my children to dote on. It is easy to see why people destroy themselves while in this condition: it steals your soul.

The Korean Police Action, so called by President Truman, started and took me away from Florida. I was sent to the battleship USS New Jersey. It was here that I hit rock bottom emotionally. The melodramatic scenes of throwing Catholic medals in the ocean and saying 'I don't believe in God anymore' occurred so often with some sailors that I would not be surprised if the ocean rose a couple of feet. We all went to Mass aboard ship the following Sunday and bought another medal. Ah, what tormented romantic souls we were!

I fell in love with Japan (if falling in love with a country is possible) at first sight. And what a sight it was. Just at early dusk, the ship arrived in Tokyo Bay, just outside of Yokosuka. There is a moderately high mountain just behind the city. As the sun went down, the lights in the lower city were lit, and as the sun gradually went farther down, the lights went on up the mountain. I had wanted to go to Japan since grade school when I saw pictures of the quaint houses with paper walls. Now I was here.

SCHLITZ BEER

Going on shore leave was the event of a lifetime. Walking the narrow streets with many kiosks was totally new to me, and I loved it. In the poorly lit streets, items in the kiosks looked alluring. I saw a standing metal crucifix about six inches high. I had to have it, so bought it. When I returned to the ship that night, I looked closely at it in the bright lights. What a surprise! I thought it was silvered plated but it was only silver paint. I turned it over and saw the words Schlitz on the bottom of the stand. I kept it for many years before it was lost in moving around.

We went to sea for Korea, and returned to Yokosuka after a month or so each time. I hated to leave Japan, but I was ready to come home. Little did I know what the future held for me in Japan.

After sea duty I saw no good reason to stay in the Navy, so I took my discharge when my four years were up. After awhile, I got tired of being home and the wanderlust for the military set in. But not for the Navy. Another stint at sea would have destroyed me. I joined the Air Force.

Chapter Five

Air Force Duty

My first duty station in the Air Force was at Donaldson AF Base in Greenville, South Carolina. Another small band in a quasi-county club. We golfed, played tennis, and all those things which bands do in the military. I met some friends there, one in particular, who has been my friend ever since. There were no great events in Greenville. Only some of the most interesting personalities I ever met. I thought the Navy had some unique people, and it did. But harbored in that small band of about 20 Airmen, there were, by percentage per capita, more unique people than in the Navy bands. And that is saying a lot.

I requested a transfer to Berlin, but instead was assigned to Tokyo. What was to be the beginning of some semblance of normalcy in my life was to meet the lovely lady, Kumi, that was to be my first wife. We were married in Tokyo. It took a little doing as, for military personnel, marriage with Japanese was frowned upon, and marriage to a foreigner was taboo for the Japanese, especially with the upper crust as her family was. I was there from 1955 to 1957, and married in 1956.

We returned to America and stationed first near Kansas City, Missouri where my son was born, then transferred to Colorado Springs, CO, where my daughter was born. My wife took ill, so I had to quit the Air Force, after six years, because I traveled a lot with the NORAD Command Band and she could not drive. We moved to California. During this time, we had great financial difficulties. Trying to feed a hungry family when no regular, permanent job is available, will force a person to earn money in many various part time jobs. Eventually, after many failures, I found a regular job so the part time jobs ceased.

We returned to Japan in 1962. My wife died in 1963. She was Roman Catholic so received the last rites. Cremation is required in the cities.

THE LAST TOUCH OF LOVE

The ceremony of cremation is the strangest event I have ever witnessed. There is a three-day wake at home. Immediately after the Requiem Mass at the Church, her body is taken to the crematorium where the plain pine coffin is set on a gurney. The room is a large open space, dirt floor, with some pictures of Buddha on the wall. I am given a nail and a rock about the size of a baseball. It was gestured to me that I should drive the first nail into the lid of the coffin. After I did so, family and friends came forward to finish the job. The box is then rolled to the oven and the box is pushed in. The door is slammed shut. There are two padlocks with one key each. After the door is secured with one of the locks, the key was given to me. The key to the other lock is kept by the undertaker. We wait about an hour in a small, but beautiful, room just a few steps from the crematorium where we sit on cushions on the floor, talk quietly, drink delicious green tea, and eat very small sweet cakes (more like firm jello). We are called back to the room. The door is open and I see for the first time a cremated body. There are a few ashes, but they are of no importance. The bones are important. A ceramic jar, about the size of a crock-pot, is placed on a small table on my right side as I stand at the head of the metal tray containing small, but discernable, pieces of her skeleton. One of her friends picks up a small bone at her feet and then passes it to the person next to her with chopsticks (this is the only time that things are passed from chopstick to chopstick). Slowly, respectfully, one person at a time, on either side of the table, continues the procedure and all of the pieces are passed to me and I place them in the jar. At last, (finally before I pass out) the last piece of bone showing is a small round piece of her skull. I pick that up and put it in the jar. This is the last touch I had with my love. The jar is placed in a wood box and the whole thing is wrapped up in a white bandana type of cloth. It is given to me and we returned home.

Later the remains are buried in the cemetery. After about 40 days of the remains having been placed in the small family altar, several of us climb into a few taxicabs and take her remains to the cemetery.

THE CROSS CARRIER

Earlier I had an almost full sized wooden cross made to put at her grave site. The shop for the head stones, where the cross was made, was across the street from the cemetery. The cross was too big to put into the taxi to carry it to the grave site, about 10 minute walk. I started to carry the cross, but one of her male relatives insisted he carry it. It would be unseemly for the widower to carry it. The rest of us went to the gravesite and waited for the man with the cross. Shortly, we saw him carrying the cross over his shoulder, just as pictures showing Christ doing it. Since it was a large cross, and he was short of statue (but large indeed in charity and dignity), the bottom of the crossbeam bounced off the ground as he walked. All of us at once did what we could to keep from laughing at this Buddhist carrying the cross of Christ in a Christ-like manner. He, being the perfect gentleman and good Japanese, did not loose his perfect inscrutable Oriental demeanor. Perceiving the situation, he laughed first. Then we men, like a broken dam, did our dignified muffled laugh, and the ladies did their hand-over-mouth giggles. It was the great comic relief for me after such a long time of sadness.

Chapter Six

Civilian Life

I married again, to Eiko, while in Japan, in 1965. I graduated from Sophia University in 1966. Living in Japan as a civilian for seven years was most certainly very different than living there in the military. It was a most sublime, and educational time. We moved back to America in 1969. I graduated from Central Missouri State University in 1972 with a Masters degree in Safety. Eventually she died of cancer in 1976 in Fargo, North Dakota. Both wives died after a long bout with unbelievable pain from cancer. No matter how much advance notice and preparation you have before the final moment, it is still a shock and emotionally draining when the end finally comes. The memory of the suffering and deterioration from a being a beautiful woman to become, literally, skin and bones, is still with me today, 40 years later for the first wife, Kumi, and 28 years after the second wife, Eiko.

A KISS UPON HER LIPS

Hoping to get a nap, I nestle my head in my arms on the side of the bed by my wife. There she lay, emaciated, wracked with cancer, with the pallor of death creeping over her face, and to me just as beautiful as ever. My nap is fitful and tormented; I drool a little on the sheets. The hospital falls into the evening routine, finally letting the patients sleep. Visitors leave, except those like me, waiting for the ultimate Visitor. At our wedding, 11 years earlier, I promised to love and protect her through sickness and in health, in the good times and in the bad times. That I do now, and suffering with her, until the inevitable occurs. In that twilight state between sleep and awake, a veiled dream of the past years' events appear.

Eiko, an excellent pianist, played Chopin, Schumann, Beethoven, Ravel,

Debussy, and many other composers. She often practiced instead of cooking dinner, and that was all right with me; many evenings she played for me. For a few months now I knew her health was failing, because she practiced less often. Another hobby of hers was sewing. She sewed almost everything. A couple of years earlier, for a Christmas party, she made a gorgeous evening gown of brocade silk, a long skirt and matching vest; it rustled as she walked. It was mostly black with multi-color threads entwined through out. She bought a pastel yellow blouse with frills on the front and cuffs. The blouse matched the yellow threads in the faintly outlined dragons in the material. The black dragons, a shade or two darker than the material, were barely visible, and that, with black patent leather shoes, made it all the more beautiful. All together, with her black hair, oriental features, and complexion was a stunning ensemble. The ensemble was very expensive, which was a rarity for her to spend money on herself. She wanted to look great for the annual company Christmas party when we lived in Wichita, Kansas. She did not look only great, but fantastic! Many women, and men, admired her looks. Then they admired her even more when it was discovered she made the dress and vest herself.

She woke me up, that unforgettable morning of despair a few years later in North Dakota, showing me that her stomach had swollen as if a grapefruit had grown inside her. I took her to the closest hospital, 15 miles away. They removed the tumor the next morning. As soon as she was able to travel, I took her to a hospital in Fargo, ND. They started chemotherapy and radiation treatments hopefully to cure her cancer. After awhile they sent her home, hoping the treatments were successful.

Gradually she improved, but remained slightly weak. She always wanted a Grand Piano, but never bought one; she thought it cost too much. I convinced her we could afford it, so we traded in the studio upright for a new Baby Grand. She loved that piano, and played it often when she had the strength.

In less than a year, she hardly played it any more. I took her back to the hospital in Fargo. She was in and out of the hospital a few times, every week or so. The doctors hesitantly told me that she should stay for an extended period of time. That aroused my suspicions even more. Was it incurable? Would she die? They confirmed it. They did not know how long it would be, but they would do all they could for her. How would they keep trying?

There were needles in her ankles, needles in her legs, needles in her arms, needles in her wrists, and needles in her hands. She was a living, agonizing, pincushion. Her hair fell out, so I bought her a wig; she wanted it, but then refused to wear it; she wore a bandanna instead. She never weighed more than 110 pounds, now she barely weighed 70 pounds. She was literally skin and bones. Even with all of that, she was beautiful to me.

One day I received a telephone call from the doctor. He asked if I would come up to Fargo and talk to my wife about something. I asked what the problem was. He told me that she had removed all the needles and said she wanted to die. She could not bare the pain and tolerate being in bed all the time. The doctor confided in me that they were trying some experimental drugs on her and needed a little more time to see how the cancer would react. He said they needed at least one more week, so would I try getting her to keep the needles in one more week? This was an extremely difficult request. I talked to her. We already discussed this very problem years before, and again recently. We agreed to let nature take its course without heroics, only to insure that the other is kept painless.

Several times she said she wanted to die. She begged me to help her die. I couldn't do it, I didn't have the facility or the know how. In any event, how could I kill the one I loved! I can understand why people do that. Yet, seeing Eiko suffer so much wrenched my very soul. Be it ever so frail, my last grip on sanity was the hope that nature must end her plight very soon.

I went to the hospital that day and talked to her. I told her what the physicians asked me to do. She asked if it were her decision. I said yes and that I would honor her decision, with no further discussion. After a moment's consideration, she agreed, but only one week, for science and humanity. I stayed while they stuck the needles into her. The next week I was there when they took the needles out. She felt a great sense of relief; it showed on her face. She knew that all the pain would soon be over. I stayed for awhile and then went home. My son and I lived about an hour from Fargo, but I still visited every few days. A couple of weeks later, or maybe less, the hospital gave me a call at work. The doctor told me I must get to the hospital that day.

I went directly to the hospital from work, but she lingered on for several days. I wished I had brought more clothes with me. Later, after wearing the same clothes all that time, I threw them away. She was still conscious and glad to see me. She knew she was fading quickly. My son had gone to see her a few times. She was glad to see him those times, but glad that I didn't bring him at this particular time. She asked earlier that I not bring him; she wanted to be remembered as she used to be.

When awake, her mind was clear and she spoke English fluently. She never lapsed in to Japanese during the whole year of suffering. I stayed by her side day and night, so I began to get a little dizzy. I needed to walk and stretch for a few minutes. As she slept, I told the nurse I was going outside for a moment. It was August, a very beautiful evening. Walking around the block, I passed a couple of ladies, sitting on a bench under a street light. I greeted them. They, responding in kind, commented about my accent and asked where I was from. I told them and we talked a bit about the weather. They asked what I was doing in Fargo. They had to be about 60 years old, dressed in nondescript dark dresses with ugly, black, laced up shoes. Their feet barely touched the pavement as they sat there. They were like old hens sitting on their nests. I stood there in all innocence telling them what I was doing. Without the slightest hesitation, one of them said how lonely I must be, and the other one wondered, aloud, about going to bed with them, for a price, of course. So there it was, with my wife on her death bed only half a block away, I was hustled by a couple of over-the-hill hookers. What to do in such a case? Declining their invitation and walking away, I started laughing. It was a marvelous laugh and I felt better for a moment. I couldn't be angry with them, I realized they had their problems, too.

I returned to her bedside after being propositioned. A couple of days later, in the early morning of August 10th, 1976, with the sun brightly shinning, she laid her hand on my head. I had not moved my head away from the bedside all night during the fitful dreams. She had put her hand on my head a little earlier. Her hand slipped off my head. I roused out of my stupor, wiped the drool from my lips, and realized that I had been sleeping and dreaming of the events of our lives together. I raised up, taking her hand into mine. That hand was now black and blue, bruised by the feeble efforts of modern medical science. I held the hand that was used as a pincushion, used as a dutiful wife caring for me and my son when we were sick, used to play the piano, used to cook my meals, used to sew suits for me and my son, used to hold my hand affectionately, used that hand while she, in sheer agony, gave an extra week to humanity. That hand gave my hand a slight squeeze, then relaxed. Looking into her face, I saw an expression of complete contentment. The nurse came in and searched for a pulse that wasn't there. My love slipped away. She was now at peace. I was left, once again, alone without a love of my own. The nurses were so kind through it all, and now the final act was a true act of kindness and mercy. She raised my wife's head up, took the pillow from under her, fluffed up the pillow and replaced it. She straightened out my wife's few strands of hair and tucked the covers under her chin. My wife looked very comfortable and serene, beautiful, and peaceful. I looked at her for a moment, again thinking briefly, of the good and hard times we had during our 11 years of marriage. There lay a true folk heroine (earthly saint?), I thought.

Then I leaned over and placed a kiss upon her lips. Was that the millionth, or the millionth and one we gave each other? She was buried in the brocade silk evening gown, and the wig, and was just as stunning as at the party.

Because of many reasons, I could not end the pain for my wives, for which they pleaded most pitifully.

Drifting from one job to another, again with the codependency in full swing, I finally found myself in Minneapolis, MN.. Many accomplishments were made in the 20 years I have lived here. Marathons, half-marathons, triathlons, weigh lifting, teaching aerobics on my 60th birthday, and retirement from the Veterans Affairs Hospital. This is the end of the beginning. Now we go to the beginning of the Great Beginning of my new life: finding Christ.

Chapter Seven

Theosis

The most amazing things happen when least expected. There I was, washing dishes and listening to the radio. I heard the commercial for the beginning of a new semester at the Alfred Adler Graduate School of Psychology. This was June 1998. I responded to the advertisement and called the school. After discussions at the school, I was accepted. I started classes in August. In time, I needed practical supervised experience for credits. I was advised to contact a hospice as a volunteer. I started the training as a volunteer on February 16, 1999. Part of the group training was a session with the Chief Chaplain. You know how it is when you meet someone for the first time and right away you are friends? Well, that is how it was between the Chief and me. We became close friends and have remained so ever since. Peter, I discovered, was a Bishop in a continuing Anglican Church. As I did my volunteer work, we became more friendly. He asked me many questions about my spiritually and Church history. He must have sensed spiritual stirrings within me. About this time I had a dream that I did not understand for several months. The dream was that I was being chased by little devils, hundreds of them. I was crying out for help when St. Michael the Archangel appeared and fought off the devils. I felt better spiritually about it. Those I told about it just shook their heads. Now they probably do not even remember I told them about it.

April 1999 found me volunteering at a home for people with Alzheimer's and dementia as an Eucharistic Minister and spiritual leader. I stayed there for two years and two months, during which time I was ordained a deacon, priest and consecrated an Abbot with Apostolic Orders.

As yet I was still not at ease with my spirituality. Something was missing. Then in May 22, 1999 I was received into the Company of Jesus Order in Mankato, Minnesota. This is a small interdenominational organization founded by Bishop Peter. Another person was ordained a deacon at the same time. Later he and I became close friends. This was a great experience. Still, I was not totally at ease spiritually. The next day, I was at a retreat in Collegeville, Minnesota, for Chaplains and personnel of the hospice. This is a retreat house run by the Benedictines. The ecclesiastical group that Peter belonged to was a Vineyard Convergent organization claiming Apostolic succession. An Archbishop, former Roman Catholic priest, from the group, was in Minneapolis to conduct the retreat. After the Celebration of the Eucharist, the Archbishop had a healing service. I personally am not much into unsubstantiated physical healing, but I stayed with it. Suddenly, as the Archbishop stated that healing of the soul is a healing of hurt, despair, loneliness, and sins never having received forgiveness. He called all those to be healed of body or soul to come forward. I was called. Being in a kind of blind and mental stupor I was hardly even aware of what I was doing. I rose from my seat walked slowly forward and faced the Archbishop. When he asked what healing I needed, without knowing why nor how, I said, "Healing of my soul." He laid his hands on my head and gave absolution. I began to weep uncontrollably for 30 minutes. There were no bright lights, singing angels, ringing bells, phenomena, terrestrial, or otherwise. There was only me, basking in the light of Christ's compassion and forgiveness.

I was now at peace with my Redeemer. There was no turning back. The Holy Spirit captured me. My soul, which had been held in bondage by Satan for decades, was once again redeemed by Christ and returned to me: I again had the power of choice which Satan denied me. This is my claim to theosis, deification, transfiguration, revelation. From that moment, I was a changed man!

After that, I also became a Chaplain for the hospice where I was a volunteer. In one stage or another, all patients in the hospice program were dying, supposedly in about six months. Some took over a year, but there was a continuous deterioration. Some of them died before I arrived to where they were; others took from and hour or longer. None of the visits was the same. Here are the most memorable.

A COMPASSIONATE CHAPLAIN

I was sent to a nursing home to minister to a person who was actively dying, i.e., could die at any minute. When I reached the nursing home I look at the patient's record to see what his denomination was. There was no information about that. I asked the nurse if she knew. Her reply was that the family did not state it and wanted nothing more to do with him; a young man about 25 years old. She informed me that they said something to the effect that when he died do not inform them as they didn't care. For the burial, just dig a hole and throw him in it. He had been a drug addict for several years and a real thorn in the side of the family.

I went to his room and found him on a bed mattress that was on the floor. He was literally skin and bones with tattoos on his arms. I touched his arm to see if he were still alive. He was. He pulled his arm away from my touch. I talked to him but received no reply. Not considering myself anything of a theologian, I fell upon my experience of suffering and did what I though was compassionate, for that is what Christ taught us to be to each other. I could not believe that a person who suffered so severely did not, some time in his life did not say he was sorry and wished that God would help him. We should not limit the mystical, infinite, Divinity to conform to our concept of time and space. Therefore, as we are taught, the Crucifixion and redemption of Christ was, is, continually exists yesterday, today, and tomorrow. From that perspective, I took the holy oil, holy water, and Eucharist along with the prayer book from my kit. I proceeded to bless him with holy water and anoint with holy oils. Then I touched the

Eucharist to his lips and consumed it myself for him. Theologically, canonically, correct? I don't know. What I do know is that hopefully I helped another sinner, such as I am, to be redeemed by our most compassionate Redeemer. That is what I would want someone to do for me.

SUICIDE

As I walk into the funeral home, I am approached by the Funeral Director. He informs me the deceased committed suicide and the family is quite distraught. He further informs me they will ask me to do something quite extraordinary. Indeed they did. They said the man was a good person. He was generous, considerate and a good husband, father, and brother. The problem is that he was a weak person when it came to alcohol and drugs. They wanted to know, since his church would not give him a funeral, could I give him absolution. For a very brief moment, I hold their broken hearts in my hand. I could deny their request and shatter their already broken hearts. But that is not in my nature. I granted their request, and just as though he were in confession, I absolve him of his sins. I anoint him with holy oil and sprinkle him with holy water. I invite the family members to sprinkle him with holy water. After the final hymns and prayers, I close the service. The families are in tears of joy. I did that for the family as the deceased is in the care of the Compassionate Lord Jesus. I do not have the heart of a cold theologian insisting the law be observed. If what I did was wrong, I beg the Lord to forgive me for being compassionate to a suffering family.

A Matter of Title

Another situation is not quite so gruesome. I was sent to a high rise for seniors to visit another actively dying person: an elderly lady. I was greeted at the door by a lovely young lady who was taking care of the older lady. The apartment was nicely kept as well as the dying lady as she lay in bed. The young lady said the other lady was her grandmother-in-law. The patient appeared to be asleep, so I said that I would quietly say some prayers and leave. The young lady said the patient was not asleep, just had her eyes closed. I commented that I would like to talk to her. The young lady said, "Grandma, the Chaplain is here". No response. Then she said, "Grandma, Father Bob is here." No response. Finally she said, "Grandma, Pastor Bob is here." Here eyes immediately opened wide and she thanked me and asked for prayers, then closed her eyes again as though sleeping. The patient was a Lutheran, and Pastor was the only title she would honor.

The Burial Stole

There were times when I was ministered to, rather than ministering to others. One case in particular was with Katie Mae. She was a black lady from the south. She lived near my house so visited her often for about a year. Katie Mae accepted many denominations. She had a large statue of the Blessed Virgin with rosaries hanging on it. She belonged to a Baptist Church. When I visited her, we would sing many of the old Spirituals. She knew many that I had forgotten.

Sometimes she made up her own. The hospice also had a Music Therapist which, together, we would visit Katie Mae. We prayed with her, just talked to her, and always sang hymns. She really liked to be blessed with holy water, anointed with holy oil, and receive Communion. Several times, I let her bless and anoint me. A few weeks before the end of her life, I asked her if she would like to give me Communion. She was thrilled at the thought. She said she was not ordained so couldn't give me Communion. I asked her if she would like to be ordained. She was so excited that she could hardly speak to say yes. I placed my hands on her head, and ordained her. I took off my stole, put it around her neck, and I asked her to bless me. She asked me saying, that, "Now it was not just Katie Mae, but Reverend Katie Mae that blesses me?" I assured her that was true. She laid her hands on me blessing me, and gave me Communion then and a few times after that. I gave her my stole. A family member hid the stole from her for whatever the reason. I gave her another one with which she was buried, at her request. The family requested that I say a few words at the funeral since I had met most of them. A Baptist preacher, a large black man was the primary officiating minister. I said a few words of happiness for having known her, being discreet and careful not to over do it. Afterwards, the Baptist preacher and I embraced, showing respect to the memory of Katie Mae, and each other.

APPLE JUICE

At another nursing home, I ministered to a lady who was a Pentecostal. She often asked to be blessed with holy water, anointed with oil, and receive Communion. One day she commented that I never used wine with Communion, and she liked the intiction method, that is, the Host dipped into the wine. I told her that in the summer the wine would quickly turn into vinegar, so I didn't bring any. Without the slightest hesitation, she pointed to a glass and said, "There is some apple juice, a natural juice like wine. Having ministered to her for several months, I knew better than to discuss it with her. So, I consecrated the apple juice and gave her Communion with it.

As with the first example, I don't know how canonically correct or valid my acts were, but I was a Christian Minister, and we are supposed to, within reason, be charitable. In any case, I was a compassionate Chaplain and pray that God will be the same with me.

DEATH BED BAPTISM

For several months I visited a little older than middle aged gentleman in a nursing home. He had suffered all the pitfalls of a dysfunctional marriage and divorce, partly, but not completely, estranged children, and what else I don't know. He was fairly talented with leather working, making wallets, key rings, and the regular assortment of leather goods. His real masterpiece was a large engraving about four feet by one foot, work of the Last Supper. It was truly a beautiful piece of folk art. I would listen to his music of country records of the 50s and 60s with him. I personally do not care for that kind of music, but I was there for his benefit, not mine. Finally, after he was out of denial and admitted he was dying, and that it would be very soon, he said, "Father, I don't ever remember being baptized." Now, to a devoted Christian as I hope I am, this is a very powerful statement. Unless you want to be baptized, it is best not say that. I was forbidden to ever ask about things like that so I never inquired. But, since he opened the door, I asked if he wanted to be baptized. He said he did. I immediately recruited a nurse, open my black bag of sacramentals (and sacraments). We briefly talked about his life and was sorry for his sins and forgave those who offended him. I took out the holy water, oil, Eucharist, and Baptism Service Book and proceed to baptize him, anoint him, and give him Communion. He, like the thief on the right side of Jesus at His crucifixion, received his redemption at the last minute. He died a few hours later. His family was ecstatic concerning his baptism. The nursing staff was extremely happy about it as they had grown fond of him. It was not the classic, in church, baptism, but better than not at all.

Little did I know at that time how truly great the experience was.

Being saved, slain by the Holy Spirit, transfigured, and to be authentic, requires a life change. It would take several pages to give the litany of changes in my lifestyle. A lifestyle change is one of the most difficult accomplishments a person can do. A few of the many changes were discarding all my expensive jewelry and giving the pieces to my son as heirlooms; stopped dying my hair; stopped dressing outlandishly; stopped hanging out at the old haunts on the 'Strip' (series of pick-up bars on one of the major interstates); stopped cruising the seedy, sleazy, sinful section of downtown Minneapolis; started getting out of codependency relationships, stopped feeling sorry for myself, etc. Although I was physically among the hurting, downtrodden masses of God's living icons, doing what they did, saying what they said, in the depths of my soul I did not feel as belonging there; but for the grace of God, there go I. It was a few weeks later I asked my physician to let me stop taking antidepressants. He agreed, but with the stern advice that if I were to become depressed again, I would contact him immediately. I agreed, but I felt better without the medication than I did with it, and have not taken any since then. I tried a year or so before this time to do without the medication, but had to resume taking it.

My metamorphosis was overnight. Truly, 'His yoke is easy and His burden is light'. However, there are times when I had rather sleep in on Sunday mornings, or other days, when I should be in Church. It is difficult sometimes to force myself to get dressed and go. There are times I miss the bars and the so-called 'camaraderie' with other drunks and misfits. Should anyone think that the times and kinds of sin equal to those of Biblical times are extant no longer, you are sadly mistaken. It happens all day and night, everyday and night. The sins for which Christ forgave the two women are not confined to women. Men, too, commit adultery and sins of all kinds. Not much, if anything, is said about suffering after forgiveness from Christ Himself, or even today. Knowing what it is to give up one lifestyle for another, I can sympathize with them. In their secret hearts, they must have suffered horribly, just as we do. God remembers not our sins (Isaiah 44:25), but we remember them. Not only remember them, but constantly tempted by them. Not only tempted by them, but influenced by them. Every decision we make every minute of everyday, every relationship with every person is, to some degree, clouded by the memories of them. The fear and doubt that we cannot be loved, or liked, by particular people without some kind of dependency on them, trying to please them, trying to buy their friendship and loyalty with money or some other way, or sinning with them, is forever with us. This constant cloud over our heads, awake or in dreams while sleeping, gives us no rest. There are times when Satan sends whirlwinds of temptations and memories that are almost overwhelming. Except for the grace of God, I would lose spiritual consciousness and succumb to the temptations. If remembering the sins, and that always brings temptations, is so devastatingly painful, why do we repent if repentance does not bring relief? Because this depth of despair lasts for only a little while, whereas sinning is constant with no relief. There is a saying that when we reach the end of our rope, we should tie a knot and hang on. When I am beseeched by Satan and his legions of evil minions, I hold tight to my prayer rope, pray the Jesus prayer and other prayers. Soon Satan is again defeated and the onslaught ends. The relief that I have sinned again gives me release as well: I don't have to feel guilty over another sin. Another person just like me, but unknown to you, could be next to you in church, ahead of you in the Holy Communion line. But it is the glory of the Redeemer that the person is there. Is it possible? Is it conceivably possible? Is it at all possible, with Christ's understanding of Mary Magdalene's mental torture, she remembering her demons. He knows our mental torture as we remember our demons, that He chose her as the first person to reveal Himself after the Resurrection? This would be very consistent with the behavior of a close friend of a person like Mary Magdalene. This would give her the feeling of really being accepted, as she is, not as she was, and trusted with a highly important mission. It would be a singular, unique, act of Christ's devotion to her; an act that could be done only once, and she was chosen. When we remember our sins, we must remember that Christ gave a unique act for us as well: His crucifixion.

Therefore, when I am tempted by my past lifestyle, all I have to do is think of the agony of the former life and compare it to the joy of my new life, and I find the burden of the Redeemer is lighter beyond compare. Further, remembering the past misery is not the same as experiencing it again. Although we are forgiven our sins, we are not expiated from the civil consequences if they were criminal as well as sinful. The guilt we have for criminal acts is of God, because all just laws come from God, but what we do about it is guilt of our own making. If, then, we still suffer the misery of remembering, why should change our lifestyle? Christ tells us (Mark 10: 17-22) to, "...sell whatsoever thou hast…take up the cross, and follow me." By selling our possessions does not mean just our land, jewelry, etc., but also to deny ourselves of our sins. Our sins are of great value to us, otherwise we would not fight so hard to maintain them: that burden is much heavier than the cross of salvation. Because once we have repented, i.e., changed our thinking, changed our lifestyle, begged God's mercy and forgiveness, and been forgiven we become more God like, returning to our original state of creation: created in God's image and likeness. Then we will have the strength and grace to not repeat the sins again. That is the light burden of Christ. Otherwise we doom ourselves to live the misery of sin for the rest of our life. There is always hope, through faith, prayer, good works, and the grace of God, that our memories will become dimmer and less powerful over time.

However, there was still a longing for just a little bit more; I was not yet, complete, even after the conversion. I needed a parish to belong to. I tried the Episcopal Church, but that wasn't quite right. I considered going back to Catholicism, but ruled that out because I was a pre Vatican II Roman Catholic. Bishop Peter did not have a parish, as such, in the traditional sense. There was one small parish in Mankato of fromer Episcopalians who needed a parish priest. So for awhile I traveled there once a month to Celebrate the Eucharist. That was great, but still not just right for me. I finally found what I was looking for by accident.

I greatly enjoy riding my bicycle. On. May 5, 2001 I was biking around my neighborhood when I noticed a church called Orthodox. I didn't know exactly what that was, but I did know it was an ancient church, something like the Roman Catholic Church.

THE PEARL OF GREAT PRICE
It was mid afternoon when I saw the marquee that vespers was at 5 p.m. So I decided to go. The anticipation was greatly rewarded when I walked into St. Herman's (Russian) Orthodox Church (OCA). I knew then that I had found what I was looking for.

The mysterious and beautiful Icons, the smell of incense, bells, the candles (smells and bells without the yells as it is sometimes referred to) all touched my inner self and the search for a home to replace the former life was complete. I had been touched by the Divine, and now discovered the home that He founded, the Pearl of Great Price, in which to rejoice. My home now is in Jesus the Christ and His Church. I no longer have to force myself to go to Divine Liturgy and other services, I want to go and eagerly wait until it is time to go again.

Most truly my theosis, transfiguration, is not as magnificent and glorious as that of Moses' on Mount Sinai, Jesus' on Mount Tabor, or the Apostles and others at Pentecost, or great saints in history. Even against all my scorners, those who sneer at me, defamers, and disclaimers that said it could not have happened to someone like me, I reply, it is my experience, my lifestyle change, and my redemption: it is my own little theosis to claim and for no one else to judge. By the grace of God I will not betray that touch with the

Divine, regardless how slight, or wispy, or glancing it was.

"...forgive us our trespasses as we forgive those who trespass against us...." Many people, and many times, have done grievous and heinous harm to me, by either word or deed. As You have commanded, gracious Lord, without reservations or conditions, with all my heart, mind, and soul I do forgive them and pray for them. All those whom I have harmed by word or deed, I most humbly beg they search their hearts for charity and compassion and forgive me.

Should anyone think that I am claiming to have become a living saint after the experience is sadly mistaken. I am still tempted by the memories of the past. I have flashbacks from the time in the fields of flowers and bees, through all the time in between until now. The difference between the time past and my theosis is the acute awareness of the love, compassion, and redemption of our Lord. Now I have the strength, courage and faith to live for Christ and the Church, albeit an imperfect life.

"...since you are the Theotokos...accept this prayer from my impure lips and with the power of your maternity, beg your Son, my Lord and God, to open for me the depths of His loving kindness, forgive me countless sins, convert me to true repentance, and make me faithful to His commands: You who are compassionate, be my constant companion." (From the Compline)

Chapter Eight

The Sports Arena

'There is no fool like and old fool.' I do not know who said that first, but it is so correct, at least for me. Out of sheer vanity and desperation to stay in the 'youth group' as long as possible, I joined a health club in 1984, at 54 years old. I deceived myself by believing the hype about being young again if only I would work out. And, not just at any health club, but each one of them says that it is the best; from the best I will get a bigger bang for the buck. Actually, you will get out of anything what you put into it, regardless of what the activity it is or which health club you join.

Doing the right thing for the wrong reasons will still give the same results as doing the right thing for the right reason. Therefore, regardless of why I exercised, I got the same physical results. It did not get me what I wanted, to recapture my youth. That was true denial of reality to think I could do that, but I did greatly improve my health. Lifting weights, a little aerobics exercise, and a reasonable diet did wonders for this aging body, i.e., tone my sagging muscles, flatten my tummy, and give me more strength and energy. The only drawback was, because it enhanced my physical appearance, gave me more energy, and stamina, it also helped me get deeper into the mire of sin. It did not restore my youth, but I thought it did. My self image was improved from one perspective, but not for the real me. It was an improvement for a fantasized me, what I fooled myself into believing what I wanted to believe: that I was young again so had the alluring power of youth. What I did was to alienate myself from many people of good character.

There were a few people, regardless of my inappropriate behaviors, outlandish jewelry, dying my hair, and clothes made for the younger set, who helped me with many athletic accomplishments. I know I must have caused them great embarrassment at times, but they were brave enough to stand with me when it counted.

One day, late January 1987, I saw on T.V. and older woman teaching an aerobics class. My great pride was not to be outdone. I said to my self that I could do that. I made up my mind to do it, and would do it on my 60th birthday. I talked to my friend Kevin Foster about it. He said give it a try. I was smoking 2+ packs of cigarettes a day. I knew I couldn't smoke and teach the class. My program to quit was decided.

METAMORPHOSIS

I knew I had to be a non-smoker for at least a year before the class. So, I told myself to enjoy this year of smoking, because I was going to stop on my 58th birthday, February 20,

1988. I did so. I started working out real hard attending aerobics classes after the year of non-smoking. I had met a new friend, introduced to me by Kevin, at the health club, John K., who was teaching aerobics. John K. said he would be glad to help me with my program and teach me how to do aerobics. He did a great job for that whole year. Before I was to teach the class, I heard something about a triathlon. I suggested to John K. that we do that. He said ok and that we would start working out for it. Then I asked, "What is a triathlon?" The *explanation* was first a swim in the lake, then a biking part and lastly a run. Well, I started having second thoughts about it, but he would not let me off the hook because I had agreed. I had never run, swam very little in the town swimming pool, the last time was in 1948. Never had I been on a 10-speed bicycle. Then he really gave me the grand kicker, we had six weeks to prepare. We went to the lake where all this was to happen. I tried to run, but could only go a few steps. He grabbed my wrist and pulled me along as he ran. We would run, walk, run around the lake, about 2.6 miles circumference. I started walking in the club's pool. I walked until the bottoms of my feet were raw. Then I tried swimming a few strokes. I obtained an old 10-speed bicycle and learned how to use the gears, with John's help. In a little over one year of not smoking, with six weeks preparation, I did my first triathlon! Suffice it to say I finished.

The time was not important. I competed in seven more. A couple of years later, I convinced my friend, John Asturias to do a triathlon with me.

AN ORTHODOX CONVERT IN
TRAINING

John K. told me about a marathon in Duluth, Minnesota called Grandma's Marathon. I went with him to see it the summer of 1990. We made a promise that we would run that race the next year. Training for a 26.2 mile marathon (I had never run more than the 2.6 miles for the triathlon), was a great shock. There is a schedule of how to prepare for the whole year. It takes great dedication and perseverance to train for the whole year. Short run days, long run days, no run days were required by the schedule. In a short time I was able to run five miles. Then I realized what I had gotten myself into and needed a new mental attitude to complete the task. Many other runners going around the lake were listening to tapes or radio with head phones. I preferred listening to the birds singing, the fish splashing in the water, wind in the trees, other sounds of nature, dogs barking, children laughing and crying and my own thinking. I was still living the life of degradation, but I was still praying, which I often did when running. I began to notice that I developed a sequential running pattern. I gave words to the pattern: (left foot) discipline, (right foot) discipline, (left foot) rhythm, (right foot) rhythm). This discipline, discipline, rhythm, rhythm, later became my understanding of the Orthodox Church. The Church has the rhythm of the Great Feast Days and fast days from the birth of the Theotokos (mother of God, blessed Virgin) in September to Her Dormition (death/assumption) the following August. All of the life Christ, and the life of the Orthodox Church, is revealed and celebrated in that period of time. The rhythmic action is the scheduled feast and fast days; the discipline is the moral fortitude to persevere in that schedule. My marathon workout to the crossing of the finish line was a time of physical training, but later becoming spiritual training with the hope of salvation when crossing the finish line of life with my last step on this earth. Many were the days I was tired, almost despaired, because of my age (61 yo), and thought I could not run the marathon. Then came the discipline: take that first step in a long journey.

MOTOCYCLES AND MARATHONS

Kevin was a motorcycle racer before being a mountain bicycle racer. In mid June 1991 I went to the Brainerd (Minnesota) International Raceway World Super Bike Race. The track is seven miles long. I was to run my first marathon in a few weeks and didn't want to change my workout schedule. So, I decided to run the track before the races begin. I climbed the fence, did some stretches, set my stopwatch to time myself, and started running. It was amazing how many people shouted their encouragement as I ran by them. Grandma's Marathon is well known so I supposed they knew what I was preparing for. When running around the lakes and streets in Minneapolis the distance does not look so far. But, when I saw two miles of straight road ahead of me, it was really terrifying. I was not about to give up with all of those people watching me. Strangely enough, I didn't feel strange running the track, even if I were the only one doing it then or ever. I had several invitations for beer for after I finished working out. I didn't take them up on it because it was still early in the morning and in training.

The same is with my Church life. It takes a lot of discipline to follow the fasts and liturgies of the Orthodox Church. The training for the marathon was truly, although not known at the time, a preparation for a spiritual life in the Orthodox Church..

YOUNG BUCKS AND FRATERITY

The day for the marathon finally arrived after a year of working out. It was a rather cool morning in Duluth and I was not dressed for it. All I had was a pair of shorts and a scanty body shirt. I thought that once I began to run I would warm up. Wrong! The wind was blowing off Lake Superior from the east. Not a strong wind, but windy enough to make me shiver from cold on the one hand and sweat on the other.

As I jumped up and down and walked around to warm up just before the race started, I noticed three young bucks, in their late 20s, body builders, with magnificent bodies. They were motioning towards me and laughing because I was an old man with skinny legs and arms and a potbelly. I held my head in shame and then I knew I was out of my element. When the race began they took off like bats from hell and left me in their dust, so to speak. I started running at my own speed as I had trained. My sweet revenge occurred a few miles down the race when I saw them limping

92

as they tried to run. I passed them by, smiled and saluted them. I never saw them at the end of the race or ever again. I know our Lord said "…vengeance is Mine…." But this was too sweet to pass up. Just as I entered the outskirts of Duluth, I ran passed a fraternity house with several brothers sitting outside drinking beer. One of them shouted out to me to come over and have a beer with them. I responded, "Are you crazy? A beer right now would probably put in the hospital." His quick reply, "Me crazy? You are the one running the marathon." I finished in four hours and 55 minutes.

The Lord watches over us all, even the stupid, like me.

John K. and Kevin were employees at the health club where John A. and I worked out. My last triathlon was in the summer of 2002 after several years' hiatus from injuries. I was thrilled to do it with my son's daughter-in-law and my son: three generations of triathletes.

BY GOD'S GRACE

After working out about a year for a possible last triathlon, the day of the competition finally came. My son, Steve, and his daughter-in-law Jessica did it with me. The weather could not have been worse. Just as the first third started, the wind began to blow fiercely, creating great waves. A big black cloud, close to the earth formed over us, almost 2,000 participants. As we got into the water the lightening began, crashing all about us; the thunder was almost deafening. We persevered. The first part, swimming, was the worst part for me, and always had been. As I finally almost crawled out of the water after the ¼ mile swim, I knew the worst was over, but had a long way to go. I got on my bicycle as the rain, like hail, pelted me. Riding the bike made it all the worse and the rain really hurt me as it fell on my bare arms and legs. The 10 miles was agony, but at least the lightening and thunder had stopped. Finally reaching the transition area, I got off my bike and started running the 2½ miles. I made a vow with God that if He would heal my injuries for just the race, I would do it for His glory and in His name. To keep my promise I wrote on the back of my white bodyshirt in big black letters: GLORIA DEI. I had not run but a few yards when a big guy, the kind you want for a friend, not an enemy, ran past me and said, "You da man, you da man." When I finished the cheering crowed had dwindled to a precious few, and many of the contestants had already finished and gone. I was one of the last to cross the finish line, but at least I finished the race, and gave God His due.

John A., John K. and Kevin have been my great friends for many years through good and not so good times. Kevin taught me how to mountain bike a couple of years after I started the triathlons. He began to compete in mountain bike races, so I would sometimes go with him on the paths.

The Last Hurrah with My Shadow

The October sun shimmers on the few remaining multicolored leaves; hardly a leaf stirs in the light breeze. My friend Kevin telephones me to go mountain biking after work. Hesitating is the wrong thing to do, with Kevin. He has good reasons for you to do what he wants you to do. Unless your reasons are better not to do what he wants -a rarity indeed- you go with him. Since biking with Kevin is not unpleasant, but very enjoyable, I agree to go. There are two very good reasons to go, and only half a reason not to go. One reason to go is that I enjoy mountain biking (I bought the mountain bike a year earlier and rediscovered the joy of being a kid again). The other reason is that Kevin does everything with a devil-may-care, speed thrills and unbounded gusto: injuries are part of the game attitude. Since the terrain is rather dangerous, I did not want him to go alone. The half reason is that the temperature is on the cold side. I do not enjoy biking in the cold, but that is not a good enough excuse for Kevin (do young athletes, like Kevin, in their 30's, ever get too cold to work out?). About 4:00 p.m., we start from Kevin's house, since that is part of his training program, and biking distance to the trail.

I wear winter biking clothing to stay reasonably warm as Minneapolis can get cold this time of year. As we depart for the trail, I wonder if this is a mistake. The weather is getting colder; the sun is below its zenith, getting well on the downside of the day. However, I know it is too late to back out, so I decided to make the best of it and enjoy the ride. Fortunately that I did so as it became a spiritual experience.

The wind-chill flushed my cheeks red as I bike. We must cross a few streets and busy intersections before we reach the trail. The traffic increases as the rush hour chases on our heels. We reach the first hurdle, a five-foot deep, six-foot wide ditch, the result of roadwork. This is not a big obstacle to a real athlete like Kevin, but to a non-athlete, 62 year old man like me, jumping across it with a mountain bike in my hands takes a lot of guts, but I did it. The next challenge is a graveled hill. Sand, and rocks of all sizes, from marbles to softballs, cover the deeply rutted hill. It was once a road, but snow, runoff, and years of abandonment ravaged it. Some grooves are as much as a foot deep and six inches wide. I proceed slowly and carefully; very, very slowly and carefully do I proceed; falling would do a person real mischief. After this fun part, we reach a paved road to the trail, about a two-mile ride, by some new gorgeous homes.

At the beginning of the trail are small patches of green grass on a flat surface. Just as we pause, to bike up a slight hill, Kevin says, "Let's make this a good one, it might be our last hurrah for the year." We proceed up the hill and, reaching a path, turn and enter the woods. We are on the main trail, a tricky, turning, twisting path that goes up and down steep and terrifying hills. As usual I fall off my bike several times because I can't stay on the trail. Kevin tells me, "Look where you want to go, not where you don't want to go. Your hands will steer where you look (applicable to life?)." Surprisingly, it's true. After a trek through the woods, going up and down the hills, soaring over fallen logs, maneuvering hairpin, and V shaped curves we reach another flat area. The trees have some leaves on them, from pretty to gorgeous, with shades, hues, and color mixes seen only in nature. The trees are only a few yards away from the trail, and to the east. An unbelievably bright golden medallion hastily sets; there are no clouds or dust in the air to obstruct the sun's rays. Out of the corner of my eye, I see a figure riding along with me, going at the same speed. Being mesmerized, I think it is another biker.

I think of myself as I was years ago: large waist, with skinny arms and legs. I describe myself as a rotund Irish potato with toothpicks sticking out of it. Here, however, is a slender person biking beside me, bending over the handlebars and biking with great experience. He looks like an athlete, showing winning from as he peddles a short distance behind Kevin's shadow. I snap out of my stupor, and look again. It isn't someone else; it's my shadow. My shadow is a true likeness of myself. How proud I am! I am very close to looking as Kevin looks. I appear as though I belong there. I do belong there. I, too, am now something of an athlete. This vision of hope realized quickly vanishes, as we are in the woods again. Kevin was right, it did become the last hurrah for the year, only an hour or so, but one of life's unforgettable interludes. It was the last hurrah with my shadow. I hated seeing it end. I wanted to savor it longer and revel in the athletic feeling, but dusk was invading us, and getting very cold, crispy cold. We bike to Kevin's house, reaching there just at dark. However, I am ecstatic, and glowing inside, because I knew there is always next year!

So it is with our inner self. We perceive ourselves as being different than we really are. When we realize that we are made in the image of God, we become as God in the Spirit. We thought we did not belong to God's people from distorted perception because of our sins. Once we give ourselves to Him, then we are transformed and we perceive ourselves as belonging to the people of God, where we belong, our original state of creation.

I believe the comment that, 'when I am successful, I have many people to thank, but when I fail, I have only myself to blame'. There were many others encouraging me along the way in my many endeavors to obtain good health. But, primarily, I have my friend, Kevin Foster, to thank for his patience, while teaching me to bike in such an excellent manner. I have myself to thank for working out so diligently and courageously. Perseverance, patience, proper diet, exercise, and cross-training don't do magic, but they do accomplish miracles; I am living proof.

Some of us long distance runners are obsessed, fanatical with routines and schedules. Why? Because it works for us to train properly. My routine was to run through parts of town towards a lake to run around. The concept that a slum is not a place but an attitude is not evident. There is trash, dirty diapers, partially eaten food, used and discarded men's and women's items on the sidewalk, street and lawns of the apartments. However, even in such a place, great humility and inspiration can occur

AN ANGEL IN BLACK

She is no more than in her late 20's, very thin and average height. Her clothes are a nondescript multicolor print skirt and blouse. As I run towards her, she was smiling a broad happy smile. Her perfect white teeth, along with her beautiful face and slightly moist skin, due to the early morning humidity, gleam from the bright morning sun shinning on her face. Weakly, but determined, she made her wheelchair carry her up the slight incline. I bid her a good morning. She replies in kind and said, "Sir, would you please run an extra mile for me?" Assuring her I would, I volunteer to help her up the hill. Politely declining saying she too needs her exercise. My routine for that day was for 12 miles, but I ran 13, the extra one she requested. So, why say an angel in black when her clothes were a cheap print? That heavenly vision of strength and happiness is clothed in the black skin that God gave her. Even now, 15 years later, she inspires me.

I never saw her again. But that one time was enough to leave a lasting impression on me. She probably does not remember me. How many people have we, by our actions, inspired someone, for good

or ill, not knowing it, and don't remember the person
or actions?

Chapter Nine

THE FRIENDS INDEED

John A. was always around the health club and sometimes we worked out together. Although not directly involved in much of my training for triathlons and marathons, he constantly encouraged me to continue. John A. and Kevin played soccer together for many years. I would go watch them play and join them in the after game replays at one of the local sports bars. So I did have a lot of contact with him and we were friends.

After my transformation, John Asturias was right by my side, still encouraging and supporting me. I changed the jewelry for a big cross and wore a clerical collar all the time. Many criticized me for this. But John would defend me. After awhile, as the team and friends saw a change in my lifestyle, they changed their opinion about me. John attended my liturgies at the Alzheimer home as often as he could. Relationships drift apart because of life's changes, so I do not see Kevin or John K. much any more. But John A. is still with me.

I started attending the Orthodox Church and abandoned my Anglican orders. The Church building was formerly an old Lutheran Church, but was quite run down. John A. volunteered to do some extensive cosmetic renovation, and did a magnificent job. It took a whole summer working on it off and on. Since there was no air conditioning, it would at times get very hot and sticky, but he persevered. For Pascha (Easter) one year, he made four identical copies of tall wood standing seven candle holders. For all of this time, and gas driving his car 30 minutes to and from Church, he would not accept any payment. For my old house, one year older than I am, he installed five new basement windows and other work in the basement. Still, he would not accept payment for his time and travel. All the work he did would not have been done without him, because I could not afford to have it done. He continues to help me today.

During the time I was incapacitated from the bicycle injury and surgery, he helped me get around town shopping, lunch, and just being with me. Regardless of his religious convictions, or relationship with Christ, which I do not know, his actions speak of great humility and Christian charity. He is indeed a friend in need.

Oscar Ness, a parishioner a few years younger than I, took me under his wing when I started going to Church. He taught me how to make candles. For three years we would spend almost every Saturday morning making candles from about September until May. He became my godfather. Oscar and I spend many happy hours together laughing and talking, going shopping together, etc. When I was incapacitated with the bicycle injury, he would take me to physical therapy, doctor's appointments and other Churches for special occasions.

An excellent neighbor, two doors away, and great friend, Daryl Gudding, was constantly checking up on me while unable to get around. He would shop for my groceries. He came into the house to make sure I hadn't fallen down or had something to eat. When he did take me shopping he was patient with me and when we got home he would wait in his backyard until he saw me go into my house before he went into his. He, along with the others, and my son Steve, I was well taken care of.

MISSING

The day of the accident I was supposed to be home at 4:30 p.m. to go to a soccer game with John A. I am not home, which for me not to be punctual is extremely unusual. John and Daryl have a key to my house. They go inside but I am not there. John left to play soccer. Daryl calls my son, who works in a town several miles away, and tells him I am missing but my broken bicycle is on the front steps (two people stopped when I was injured. One person called for an ambulance and the other person took my bicycle home and left it on my front steps.). They call the police but there was no record of me in an accident. I was in the emergency room, so they couldn't find me. When I get home my son, who is highly solicitous for me, is terribly upset. A day or two later he said he wanted to talk to me about the bicycle and knowing what he was going to say, I told him to take the bike away and give it to his son. This was my fourth major accident with the bike (there were many minor and three fairly serious accidents about which he did not know), so enough was enough for my son.

Chapter Ten

A PERSONAL EXPLINATION

The disclaimers against me are nothing compared with those against God and the Bible. In my own little way I must, therefore, give a personal explanation as to the reliability concerning the historical events of the New Testament.

The theaters in my small hometown were infested with rats. I don't mean mice, I mean large rats. Today theaters are in malls, shopping centers and the like that are well cleaned and not in an environment that is a haven for rats. In the 30s the theaters opened in the front to a main street. The back door opened onto an alley where all the garbage was thrown. The garbage was not picked up as regularly as it is today. So, the rats abounded in this condition. They would sneak into the theater through the spaces where the doors were not closed tightly. While watching the movie, the rats would run across our feet. We did not like it, but it was part of the times and place we lived in.

What is the point? The point is that I was very young at that time and remember it well. Now that I am 73 years old, I can tell the story with great reliability because I was there and experienced it. I tell you this now, and you tell it to other people: the fact of the rats. The story may be embellished over time. The rats may become as big as Dobermans, bright green and pink and all sorts of distortions. The fact still remains: the rats were there. Now, as I tell you, and you tell others, and they tell their children, and it is written down for those who lived after I experienced it, the factual history is recorded as written and oral. The embellishments are greatly reduced as the story is told because the written history is barely unchanged (if treated the same as with

Scripture). So it is with Scripture. In a research by Dr. Bruce Metzger, of Princeton University he compared the works of Homer's Iliad, the Mahabharata of Hinduism, and the Christian New Testament. He found in the Iliad 746 corrupted lines, in the Mahabharata 26,000 lines corrupted, and only 40 lines corrupted in the New Testament (Dr. Don Bierle, SURPRISED BY FAITH, Emerald Books, 1992). In about the same number of years, give or take a decade or so, since I experienced the rats about 1935, and wrote this manuscript in 2004, 69 years have passed. That is approximately the same number of years between Christ's life on Earth and the writing of some of the Gospels and Epistles. Since the Crucifixion of Christ, the Seven Ecumenical Councils were held to interpret, clarify, and codify the writings of the early of the Church Fathers, primarily against heresy. Those early Fathers were the disciples of the Apostles and those oral traditions were then written by them. Those disciples had disciples, and so on until this very day and are called Bishops and Patriarchs. It is only in that

Church that has not added to, nor taken from, those decisions of the seven councils where the true faith, the true Gospels of Christ is found. From my experience and study, this is the Orthodox Church. What a pity the Protestants and the Roman Catholic Church blithely disregard two thousand years of Church Tradition. The Holy Bible, from which Protestants quote as their source of infromation concerning their belief was written, and handed down to us, by the Orthodox Church. The Orthodox Church gave us the Bible; the Bible did not give us the Church.

CHAPTER ELEVEN

Historical Christ

An autobiography is suppose to tell the story of a person's life so that people will understand, and know, the person. The good things and the bad things are usually part of the story. I have told of the good things and bad things in my life. But, to know and understand me, I must tell what I believe, literally; here is my humble belief, "...For the Lord takes pleasure in His people, and exalts the humble in salvation...." (Psalms of Praise) without any excuses or apology; this is as much me as what happened to me and what I did:

I believe in one God, the Father almighty, Maker of heaven and earth, and of all things visible and invisible. And in one Lord Jesus Christ, the Son of God, the Only-begotten, begotten of the Father before all ages. Light of Light; true God of true God; begotten not made; of one essence with the Father; by whom all things were made; who for us men and for our salvation came down from heaven, and was incarnate of the Holy Spirit and the Virgin Mary, and became man. And was crucified for us under Pontius Pilate, and suffered and was buried. And the third day He rose again, according to the Scriptures, and ascended into heaven, and sits at the right hand of the Father; and he shall come again with glory to judge the living and the dead; whose Kingdom shall have no end. And in the Holy Spirit, the Lord, the Giver of Life, who proceeds from the Father; who with the Father and the Son together is worshipped and glorified; who spoke by the prophets. In one holy, catholic, and apostolic Church. I acknowledge one baptism for the remission of sins. I look for the resurrection of the dead, and the life of the of the world to come. Amen

Plato, circa 428-347 BC, gave a perspective of reality that still influences our thinking. That teaching is known as Plato's Cave. In essence, he describes a person living in a cave all his life. His back is to the opening. As people walk by, all he can see is their shadows. To that person, reality is the shadows, not the real people, walking past the cave. Should he ever turn around and see the people, he will think of them as shadows of the real thing, i.e., the shadows on the wall of the cave. Using this in Christian religion as an allegory of Christ is not new, even if it is used in modern Churches. Questions asked today, that reflect that thinking is, 'if it were proven that Christ never lived, would you still believe in Him, or would you abandon your Christian Church?' What a loaded question! First, any 'what if' question in this context is simply trapping a person to answer a question based on a premise that it is quite likely to immediately occur, which is more likely not to happen. Even so, the answer has to be yes. Buddhism, Islam, and Hinduism are philosophies. They would exist even if were proven the founders never existed. On the other hand, without the Christ Jesus, the Holy Trinity would not exist, nor have ever existed because the Trinity is eternal, meaning always was, is, and always will be, and that is the basis of Christianity and difference between Judaism and Christianity.

The Gospel of St. John states: "In the beginning was the Word, and the Word was with God. He was in the beginning with God. All things were made through Him, and without Him nothing was made. In Him was life, and the life was the light of men. And the light shines in the darkness, and the darkness did not comprehend it (1: 1-5). How much plainer could it be that Christ was a historical fact?

Since there is so much evidence, even outside the Scriptures, that shows Christ actually lived, it is beyond comprehension to hear people, especially the ministers of Christ, allegorize Christ Jesus out of existence.

Paul Bunyon, Alice in Wonderland, The Three Little Pigs, Little Red Riding Hood, Cinderella, and Snow White are all fictitious characters and stories. Not many adults, or children either for that matter, believe that they really lived. They are nice stories, with perhaps some good moral value, but they are fictitious. To allegorize Christ is to make the life of Christ a fairytale, or folklore, or folktale.

There is a time to use metaphors, which are different from allegories. Where allegories are fictitious stories about people that never existed, such as listed above, a metaphor is usually used as an example of something that does exist. For example, old people speak of their age as in the autumn of their lives. Autumn does exist, but that expression is poetic and describes the lack of life left in them; autumn being the days before death and winter a metaphor for death; spring is the birth, the beginning of life, and in nature that is so. Summer is the age of the fullness of life: robust, full bloom, and seemingly no end, as youth think they will never die.

The Vesting of priests before celebrating the Divine Liturgy consists of prayers filled with scriptural metaphors from St. Paul's Epistle to the Ephesians 6: 13-18.

To speak of Christ as the Lamb, that is, the sacrificial Lamb, is not an allegory, but a metaphor. Lambs were sacrificial animals in the Old Testament, but Jesus, shedding His blood on the cross fulfilled, once for all time, the need for sacrificial animals' blood. Shedding blood of animals in the ancient Jewish tradition was necessary for the forgiveness of sin. One statement by Christ was, "This is my Body...this is My Blood...." He did not say this is My symbolic, metamorphic, or allegorized Body and Blood, in order to ease society's squeamish stomachs, He meant it in very real terms.

Worshiping Christ as a historical person is the only canonical and appropriate manner to worship Him. Succinctly presented here is a record of the Seven Ecumenical Councils dealing with the physical, therefore historical, Christ.

THE SEVEN ECUMENICAL COUNCILS

COUNCIL	PLACE AND DATE	DECISION
First Ecumenical Council	Nicea, Asia Minor, 325 A.D.	Fromulated the First Part of the Creed. Defining the divinity of the Son of God.
Second Ecumenical Council	Constantinople 381 A.D.	Fromulated the Second Part of the Creed, defining the divinity of the Holy Spirit.
Third Ecumenical Council	Epheus, Asia Minor 431 A.D.	Defined Christ as the Incarnate Word of God and Mary as Theotokos.
Fourth Ecumenical Council	Chalcedon, Asia Minor 451 A.D.	Defined Christ as Perfect God and Perfect God and Perfect Man in One Person.
Fifth Ecumenical Council	Constantinople II 553 A.D.	Reconfirmed the Doctrines of the Trinity and Christ.
Sixth Ecumenical Council	Constantinople III 680 A.D.	Affirmed the True Humanity of Jesus by insisting upon the reality of His Human will and action.
Qinisext Council (Trullo)	Constantinople 692 A.D.	Completed the 5th and 6th Ecumenical Councils
Seventh Ecumenical Council	Nicea, Asia Minor 787 A.D.	Affirmed the propriety of icons as genuine expressions of the Christian Faith.

From Ignatius of Antioch, in the 2nd century, through the Council of Chalcedon in 451, Christian thinkers wrestled with the logical problems presented to the Greek mind by the Christological thinking of the New Testament: If the Son is God, yet distinct from the Father, how can God be called "one"? If Jesus is divine, how can he also be human? The 2nd-century Docetists (Greek *dokein,* "to seem") maintained that the humanity of Jesus was apparent rather than real, for in Greek thought the deity was held incapable of change or suffering (see Docetism). Against them, Ignatius insisted on the reality of Jesus' flesh. The outcome was the addition to the creed of the words "born of the Virgin Mary" to safeguard Jesus' humanity (see Apostles Creed), (Christology," Microsoft(R) Encarta(R) 98 Encyclopedia.   (c) 1993-1997 Microsoft Corporation. All rights reserved.

If, in fact, Jesus were not a historical Person, then why did the Bishops of the Orthodox Church take 462 years to prove that

He was a real, Divine and Human, not an allegorized Person?

A final observation: J. M. Hussey, in The Orthodox Church in the Byzantine Empire, page 24, quotes the Sixth Council, Constantinople III, 680 A.D., "...throughout the whole course of his (Jesus Christ's) incarnate life, he made manifest his sufferings and miracles, not simply in appearance but reality." The whole Eastern Orthodox Church has spoken; the decision is final, the topic is closed. The Bishop of Rome, through his legates, was only one participant of that Council. He did not convene it, preside over it, or have the final approval. He was only one of hundreds of Bishops represented.

Conclusion

We have come along way from the Field of Memories in the early 1930s, with the simple beliefs of a child, through many a heartache, much laughter, countless unmentionable sins, theosis and, finally, the petros of faith. Although I am now 74 years old, and more educated than in my early childhood, I maintain the pure innocence of faith in God Almighty as that innerchild. "And they brought young children to Him, that He should touch them: and His disciples rebuked those that brought them. But when Jesus saw it, He was much displeased, and said unto them, suffer the little children to come unto me, and forbid them not: for of such is the kingdom of God. Verily I say unto you, whosoever shall not receive the kingdom of God as a little child, he shall not enter therein. And he took them up in his arms, put his hands upon them, and blessed them." (St Mark 10: 13-16). I have found nothing greater than that. Perhaps that, too, is my own little theosis.

With all the best and bad, the salvation and sin, the serenity and sadness, I have to agree with Bishop Fulton J. Sheen that, all in all, "<u>Life is Worth Living</u>."

The greater the sin of the sinner, the greater the glory of the Redeemer.

WITHOUT A LIFE, BORN OF
HUMAN MAN AND WOMAN, THE
VIRGIN BIRTH, CRUCIFIXION, AND
RESURRECTION OF CHRIST HAVE NO
PURPOSE OR MEANING: SUCH IS THE
NECESSITY AND GOD'S
EMPOWERMENT OF MANKIND.
THEOSIS, THERFORE, IS THE
WILLFUL AMALGAMATION OF
MANKIND WITH THE CREATOR.

ABOUT THE COVER

Using the Cross inside the Star of David is metaphorical. Prophecies in the Old Testament are of a virgin from the House of David giving birth to the Messiah. The center of the Star is the womb of the Theotokos, Mother of God, or God Bearer, if you will. From that womb, in which rested the Savior for nine months, the Savior was born. It is quite appropriate, therefore, to show the Cross of the Messiah in the Star of David.

The original concept and rough draft design is by the author. The final product is from the inspiration of Henry Wilchek III of Minneapolis, MN. He kindly volunteered to help me with this project. I owe him endless thanks and pray that God grant him many years of good health, joy, and happiness.